THE ADVENTURES OF THE DISH AND THE SPOON

Hey Diddle Diddle

The Cat and the fiddle

The Cow jumped over the moon

The little Dog laughed to see such fun

MINI GREY

JONATHAN CAPE · LONDON

Someone
put a record
on the new
record player.

It was playing
our tune.

How could we resist?

The Dish whirled around
on the moonlit ocean.

I didn't know
  where we were going,
  and I didn't care.

I knew the Dish
  would take us there.

We tried our luck
as an act in a
travelling show.

The audience loved us!

We were famous.

RITZY

THE DISH
THE & SPOON

The Dish got a taste for the high life.
We bought a motor car.
The Dish shopped for
jewellery and furs.

Soon our money
was
all
gone.

A gang
of sharp
and shady
characters
offered to
lend us some.

They tried to frighten the Dish.

What could we do?

We couldn't pay them back.

"Stop!
Untie the Dish!"
I screamed.
"I've got a plan!"

"No one will recognize us,"
  I whispered.
"Just march into the bank
  and it'll be over in
no time."

WANTED

Have you seen these two dangerous criminals?
Wanted for unarmed robbery at the City Bank
Generous reward for their capture
Contact the Police Department with information

Oh, we were so foolish!
Of course they recognized us.
We'd appeared on posters all
over the country.

We tried using
some of our old tricks
for our getaway . . .

. . . but we didn't see
that sharp rock
sticking out.

"Run while you can, Spoon," breathed the Dish.

But the Dish
was broken
and so was I.

I let them
lock me up
and turned away
from the moon.

Twenty-five years later,
I'd done my time.

I blinked in the sunny street.
The world had really changed.

What home could there be
for a lonely, broken old
spoon like me?

Then I saw this shop.
"Perfect," I said.

We DO
mend
ANYTHING

I heard a soft sobbing.
Those faded flowers
looked familiar.

rgains
alore!
ll under
wo pennies

The signs on the shelf read:

LONELY broken OLD SPOON BARGAIN 1½d

small cup lightly chipped

egg cup early view

Coffee Cup Once used The Queen

"Dish?" I whispered.
"Is that you?"
"Don't look at me, Spoon,"
she wept. "I am old and cracked,
and my glaze is crazed."

"Dish," I said, "you look just
the same as you did the
June night we ran away."

The Dish sniffed.

Someone had put
a record on the
old record player.

The sound was scratchy,
but we knew that tune.

"Can you remember the old tricks, Dish?"
I asked. The Dish nodded.
"Well, there's a whole new world out there.
People who have
never seen dishes
do tricks with
spoons."

THE ADVENTURES OF
THE DISH AND THE SPOON
A JONATHAN CAPE BOOK 0 224 07037 1

Published in Great Britain by Jonathan Cape,
an imprint of Random House Children's Books

This edition published 2006

5 7 9 10 8 6 4

Copyright © Mini Grey, 2006

To the one and only PiPPA

All rights reserved.
RANDOM HOUSE CHILDREN'S BOOKS
61–63 Uxbridge Road, London W5 5SA
A division of The Random House Group Ltd,
London, Sydney, Auckland, Johannesburg
and agencies throughout the world

The right of Mini Grey to be identified as the author of this work has been asserted in accordance with the Copyright, Designs and Patents Act 1988. THE RANDOM HOUSE GROUP Limited Reg. No. 954009 www.kidsatrandomhouse.co.uk. A CIP catalogue record for this book is available from the British Library. Printed in Malaysia.